Introduction to Fartology:
A Whiff of Science and Humor

Welcome to "**Fartology: The Science and Secrets of Passing Gas**," where we delve into the lighthearted science of farts. This book uncovers the mysteries of flatulence, from its history and cultural significance to the science behind why we toot.

Farts, a universal source of laughter, also hold fascinating scientific facts. Here, we explore everything from the impact of diet on gas production to farts in pop culture, all wrapped up with a good sense of humor. Whether you're looking for a laugh or some quirky scientific insights, this book has it all.

So, brace yourself for an amusing yet informative journey into the world of farts. Get ready to chuckle and learn – after all, everyone farts, and that's just a part of being human.

Index:

1: The Winds of History
2: Toot-torial
3: A Fluff by Any Other Name
4: The Fine Art of Flatulence
5: Gassy Gastronomy
6: Silent But Deadly
7: The Loudest Trumpet
8: Farting Fauna
9: Fart-ography
10: Fashionably Flatulent
11: Fartlek Training
12: Gone with the Wind
13: Farts in the Future
14: Toot Tunes
15: Gas-tronomy Delights
16: The Fart-chive
17: The DIY Wind Workshop
18: A Pocket Guide to Fart Jokes
19: The Grand Finale

Chapter 1:
The Winds of History: A Brief (and Cheeky) History of Farts Throughout the Ages

Whoever said, 'The more things change, the more they stay the same' was probably referring to the timeless act of passing gas. Before the first joke was ever uttered about the toots, fluffs, and poots of the world, our ancestors were already breaking wind. The history of farts is as old as the history of eating.

Let's take a windy walk through the annals of time to uncover the gusts that rustled the robes of emperors and made cavemen chuckle.

The Ancient Airs:
Egyptian hieroglyphs humorously include flatulence in scenes of daily life. In a notable carving, laborers work on a pyramid; one conspicuously bends over, others recoil in mock disgust, adding levity to their toil.

Additionally, the oldest joke from ancient Sumeria, circa 1900 BC, states: 'An unprecedented event since time immemorial; a young woman did not fart in her husband's lap.' This indicates that flatulence humor has been part of human culture since antiquity.

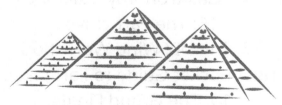

Greek Guffaws:
Ancient Greek philosopher Chrysippus is said to have died from laughing too hard at one of his own fart jokes. Now that's commitment to the craft of comedy!

Medieval Jest: The Farting Jester:
In the medieval courts, a jester cleverly used flatulence as part of his act. During a royal feast, his acrobatic flips ended with a comical toot, amusing the court and subtly mocking the aristocracy's grandeur. This act reminded all that even in solemn settings, the universal humor of an accidental fart prevailed.

Norse Winds:
In Norse mythology, the giantess Angrboða bore three children with Loki: a wolf, a serpent, and Hel, who ruled the land of the dead. It's said that Hel's realm was surrounded by a river called "Slid," whose waters were composed of swords and daggers – and it was crossed by a bridge guarded by a giantess who could be heard approaching by the loud sound of her farts.

Medieval Muffles:
The Middle Ages brought us tales of knights, dragons, and of course, flatulence. With diets rich in beans, mead, and hearty stews, those drafty castles probably echoed with more than just the howls of ghosts.

Renaissance Rips:

The intellectual and cultural blossoming of the Renaissance didn't skip over humor's low-hanging fruit. Artists and thinkers like Leonardo da Vinci and Michelangelo likely shared a chuckle or two over a particularly resonant toot.

Victorian Vapors:

The Victorians may have been prim and proper, but their tight corsets couldn't hold back nature. Rumor has it that the phrase "excuse me" was commonly used after letting one slip during a waltz.

Modern-Day Gusts:

Today, farts are a mainstay in humor, from children's jokes to blockbuster movies. Our diets, lifestyles, and even our fashion (skinny jeans, anyone?) continue to produce an array of hilarious soundtracks from down under.

In conclusion, while empires rose and fell, and fashions came and went, the humble fart remained a constant. A source of embarrassment for some and amusement for others, it's a reminder that deep down, we're all human. Or, as they say in the annals of fart history, "He who smelt it, dealt it.

Chapter 2:
Toot-torial: An Introduction to the Science and Mechanics of Farting

From tiny squeaks to mighty roars, every fart tells a story. Let's uncover the art and science behind these whimsical winds.

The Production House:
Farts begin their journey in our digestive system, where the body breaks down the food we eat. Sometimes, the breakdown process produces gasses like nitrogen, oxygen, carbon dioxide, hydrogen, and the notorious methane. It's like a mini factory inside, with gasses as the end product!

Beans, Beans, the Musical Fruit:
Ever wondered why beans lead to bountiful bouts of flatulence? It's due to the sugar molecules they contain. Our stomachs have trouble digesting them, leading these sugars to the intestines where bacteria feast on them. Their feasting results in — you guessed it — gas!

The Pressure Build-Up:
When the gasses accumulate, they increase the pressure inside our intestines. Like a balloon filling with air, there comes a point where the gas needs to find an exit. And thus, the body prepares for a toot.

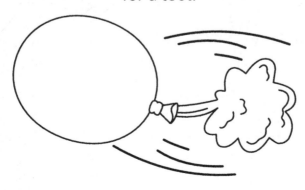

The Grand Exit:

The grand finale! The muscles in the rectum relax, allowing the gas to escape. The sound associated with this release varies. It can be silent (those sneaky ones) or akin to a trumpet's call, depending on the amount of gas and how fast it's released.

The Scent of Science:

Why the smell? Not all farts are created equal in the olfactory department. Sulphur-containing gasses like hydrogen sulfide give farts their distinct, and sometimes unpleasant, aroma. Interestingly, not all the gasses in a fart have a smell.

Farts by the Numbers:
Farts can speed out at approximately 10 feet per second!

The average person farts 10-20 times a day. That's up to 14.6 liters of gas a week! It's like our bodies are mini air pumps, providing daily, regular contributions to the atmosphere.

High Altitude Farts:
When you're on an airplane, you're more likely to fart because of the change in pressure.

The Lighter Side:
Methane and hydrogen in farts make them flammable (but trying to light one is not recommended – unless you're into singed eyebrows).

Farts in Sleep:

People often fart while they are asleep, which is completely normal.

Holding In Gas:

While it's possible to hold in a fart, it's not recommended to do so for extended periods. The gas will eventually be released, either as a fart or a burp. In extreme cases, if someone holds it in constantly, it could lead to discomfort or pain.

If you are trying to avoid the toot, avoid chewing gum. It can make you swallow more air, leading to increased flatulence.

The Social Stigma:

Despite its natural occurrence, farting is often seen as impolite. Different cultures have varied views on public toots, ranging from chuckles to sheer horror. Maybe if everyone understood the science, we'd all just laugh it off together!

In wrapping up our toot-torial, it's clear that farts, while humorous, are a natural and necessary function of our bodies. They're the culmination of complex processes, and each one tells a tale of what's happening inside us. So the next time you feel one building up, remember: it's just science in action! And maybe, just maybe, let it out with a little pride!

Chapter 3:
A Fluff by Any Other Name:
Fun Synonyms and International Words for Farts

A rose by any other name would smell as sweet... but would a fart? Journey with us as we discover the whimsical words and phrases people around the globe use to describe their cheeky cheek symphonies.

Playful English Pseudonyms:
Fluffer: A dainty, almost silent release.
Toot: Short, sweet, and to the point.
Ripper: Long, loud, and unapologetic.
Squeaker: The high-pitched cousin of the toot.
Air Biscuit: An innocent-sounding name for something potentially lethal to the nose.

International Flatulence:
French: **Pet**: As chic and sophisticated as it sounds.
Spanish: **Pedo**: A word that might make you giggle, but it's as common as saying 'fart' in English.
German: **Pfurz**: Strong and direct, just like the language.
Japanese: **Onara** (おなら): Almost musical, isn't it?
Swahili: **Kinyesi cha hewa**: Quite a mouthful for something so... airy.

Creative and Humorous Names for Farts

Whiffy Whisper, Silent Assassin, Cheeky Chirp, Puff Dragon

Thunder Clap, Sneaky Squeak, Whoopee Wind, Breezy Toot

Rumble Rouser, Hush-Hush Hum, Ghost Gust, Ninja Puff

Snicker Snort, Fluffy Pop, Gassy Gusto, Bubble Burst

Windy Wail, Cheek Flapper, Stinky Twinkle, Snort Snort

Creative and Humorous Names for Farts

Whistle Blower, Rip Roar, Balloon Burp, Tushy Trumpet

Roar Rasp, Chuckle Chuck, Booty Boomer, Hooter Honk

Muffle Mutter, Tootie Tang, Pooter Pop, Backdoor Symphony

Belly Buzzer, Bum Thunder, Whiffy Woof, Gust Giggler

Sassy Sigh, Rear Roar, Posh Puff, Breezy Blast

Historic Wind Words:

History's full of people letting them rip! Ancient civilizations had their own ways of referring to the human wind...

The Greeks had **pordé** and the Romans would giggle at a good **crepitus**.

Farts in Fiction:

From Shakespeare using "breaking wind" humorously in his plays to the iconic Whoopie Cushion making its appearance in various comedic skits, the representation of farts in media has been diverse, inventive, and ever-evolving.

The Art of Euphemisms:

Describing farts without saying 'fart' is an art in itself. "**Letting one fly**," "**Cutting the cheese**," "**Dropping an air bomb**" – the list is endless, and the creativity is commendable!

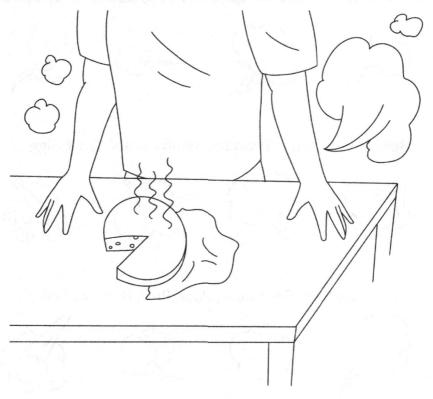

Pop Culture Pop-offs:
Blazing Saddles, remember the famous scene from the movie? Or the rhythmic fart symphony from Family Guy? Pop culture has embraced our gassy tales, naming them in hilarious ways.

Not Unique to Earth:
That stinky fart smell is not limited to Earth. On other planets, the atmospheric composition can differ. For example, the atmosphere on Jupiter and Saturn is mostly made up of hydrogen and helium, which are common components in human flatulence. While the planet Venus has clouds made up of sulfur dioxide, which, when mixed with water, would smell like rotten eggs or a really bad fart.

Words may vary and cultures might differ, but the universal act of farting and the chuckles it brings remains a constant. As we've discovered, farts have danced through languages, tiptoed across histories, and even waltzed their way into pop culture. So the next time you let one rip, think of it as your little contribution to this rich tapestry of sound and humor!

Chapter 4:
The Fine Art of Flatulence: Cultural perspectives and etiquette on passing gas around the world

From the hushed corridors of Japan's tea houses to the boisterous streets of Brazil's carnivals, the way we view, and 'do', flatulence varies dramatically. Journey with us as we traverse continents and cultures, exploring the etiquette and attitudes surrounding this most human of acts.

Japan: A Silent Tradition:

In the Land of the Rising Sun, where propriety is paramount, letting one out audibly is seen as quite impolite. Here, the subtle art of controlling one's bodily functions, especially in public settings like the traditional tea ceremony, is a valued skill. However, if an accidental slip happens, it's typically met with polite silence.

Scandinavia: Just Natural:

The practical and straightforward Scandinavians don't make much fuss about flatulence. In countries like Norway or Sweden, while it's not necessarily encouraged in public, it's seen as a natural bodily function – sometimes met with laughter, especially among friends.

Brazil: Carnival of Sounds:

In the lively streets of Brazil, especially during Carnival, the body is celebrated in all its forms. Here, flatulence might be met with a chuckle, a joke, or even a dance move. The Brazilian approach is much more relaxed compared to some other cultures.

Victorian England: The Height of Decorum:
During the prim and proper days of Victorian England, even the slightest hint of a fart was scandalous. Those who accidentally let one slip in public would be mortified, and it would be the utmost faux pas.

Maasai Tribe, Africa: A Sign of Health:
Among the Maasai, one of Africa's most well-known pastoral tribes, farting is seen as a sign of good health. It's an indication that all is well within the body, and there's no shame attached to it.

As we weave through the tapestry of global cultures, it becomes evident that our perspectives on flatulence are as varied as our languages, cuisines, and traditions. What might be a moment of mortification in one culture could be a reason for celebration in another.

The universal truth? Every culture, in its unique way, acknowledges and accommodates this natural bodily function. So next time you're traveling and feel the need to pass gas, remember: When in Rome, do as the Romans do!

Chapter 5:
Gassy Gastronomy: Foods that make you go "phhhht" and how to enjoy them

From the luscious lentils of India to the fiber-packed beans of Mexico, some of our most beloved dishes come with a windy afterthought. As we tour the world's most 'aerogenic' foods, we'll also discover tips to relish them without sounding like a deflating balloon.

Beans, Beans The Musical Fruit:
Belonging to the legume family, beans are notorious for their gas-inducing properties. This is primarily due to the oligosaccharides they contain. When these sugars reach the large intestine, they are fermented by bacteria, producing gas. Soaking beans overnight and discarding the water before cooking can help reduce their gassy effects. Enjoy your chili, but maybe not before a silent meditation retreat!

Cruciferous Vegetables:
Broccoli, cauliflower, and Brussels sprouts are nutrition-packed but can be troublesome for sensitive tummies. Their raffinose sugar content is to blame. Cooking them well can make them more digestible and less gassy.

Carbonated Drinks:

Sodas and sparkling waters introduce carbon dioxide into the stomach. While a burp is a common way to release this gas, sometimes it can find its way down and out, leading to a fizzy fart. Enjoy in moderation to avoid over-inflation!

Whole Grains:

While excellent for gut health and digestion, foods like whole wheat and bran are rich in fiber. While fiber is essential, it can also lead to gas as it ferments in the large intestine. The trick? Increase your fiber intake gradually to give your gut time to adjust.

Dairy Delights:

Lactose can be challenging for many to digest, leading to gas, bloating, and even diarrhea. If dairy products lead you to pass wind, consider lactose-free alternatives or enzymes that help digest lactose.

Onions and Garlic:

Delicious and fundamental in many dishes worldwide, these foods contain a natural sugar called fructan. If you're sensitive, it can lead to bloating and gas. Cooking them well can help, as can using garlic-infused oils instead of the raw form.

Fruits:

Apples and pears are high in fiber, fructose, and sorbitol – all of which can lead to extra gas. Cooking or baking them might reduce their gassy effects.

Tropical fruits like papaya and pineapple contain an enzyme called papain that aids in the digestion of proteins, potentially reducing gas production in the process.

Sugar Alcohols:

Found in many sugar-free gums and candies, ingredients like xylitol, sorbitol, and mannitol are not fully absorbed by the body and can lead to gas when they ferment in the large intestine.

Fermented Foods:
While they're great for gut health, foods like sauerkraut, kimchi, and some yogurts can introduce more gas into the digestive system. However, they also bring beneficial probiotics. So, the benefits might just outweigh the breezy side effects!

Ginger:
Ginger has long been used as a remedy for various gastrointestinal disturbances, including flatulence. You can chew on a piece of ginger, drink ginger tea, or include it in your meals.

Peppermint:
Peppermint contains menthol, which has an antispasmodic effect on the muscles of the digestive tract. This can help relieve bloating and gas. Peppermint tea is an easy way to incorporate it into your diet.

Fennel Seeds:
Fennel seeds are often consumed after meals in many cultures because they can aid in digestion and prevent gas. Chewing on a teaspoon of these seeds might help reduce flatulence.

Beverages:
Drinking enough water can help move food through the digestive system and prevent constipation, which can lead to gas buildup. Additionally, green tea can aid in digestion and reduce gas.

Vegetarians vs. Meat Eaters:
While one might assume meat causes more gas, vegetarian diets lead to more gas production because they are rich in fiber.

The culinary world is filled with gassy delights. While they may produce some comical sounds and sensations post-consumption, these foods also bring vital nutrients and flavors to our plates. With a little knowledge and preparation, we can continue to enjoy them without too much windy aftermath. After all, every toot has its tale and every meal its memory!

Chapter 6:
Silent But Deadly:
The mystery of odorless farts unraveled

We've all been there - a quiet room, a subtle release, and suddenly, the unmistakable stench of a fart. Yet, sometimes, even the loudest ones come with no scent at all. What's the secret behind these silent but deadly emissions? Let's delve into the science and stories of odorless farts.

The Science of Scent:
Human farts are composed of nitrogen, oxygen, carbon dioxide, hydrogen, and methane. It's the sulfur compounds (like hydrogen sulfide) that are responsible for the stink. But not all farts have the same amounts of these gasses, leading to variations in odor intensity.

Diet's Role:
Certain foods are known for producing more sulfur-rich gas. Consuming foods like meats, cauliflower, eggs, and certain beans can lead to smellier releases. On the other hand, a diet rich in carbohydrates might produce more gas, but not necessarily stinkier ones.

Silent Doesn't Mean Scentless:

It's a common misconception that quieter farts are less likely to smell. In reality, the noise of a fart depends on the volume of gas and the tightness of the sphincter muscles, not its composition. So, a silent fart can pack just as much olfactory punch as a loud one!

The Role of Gut Flora:

The unique combination of bacteria in our intestines plays a significant role in determining the smell of our gas. Some people naturally produce more sulfur-rich gasses due to their individual gut flora.

Odorless But Bountiful:

Interestingly, odorless farts tend to be more frequent. This is because they often result from swallowed air and are primarily composed of nitrogen and oxygen, which are odorless.

Medical Causes:
Certain medical conditions or medications can change the frequency and scent of farts. For instance, lactose intolerance can lead to more frequent, smelly farts, while excessive odorless gas can sometimes indicate issues with digestion.

Taming the Beast:
If you're looking to reduce the scent of your emissions, consider dietary changes. Reducing sulfur-rich foods can help. Activated charcoal tablets or certain enzyme supplements might also reduce the odor by affecting the way our bodies digest specific compounds.

The world of silent but deadly farts is a mix of biology, diet, and personal physiology. While they might be a source of amusement (or embarrassment) in our daily lives, understanding their origins helps us appreciate the intricate workings of our bodies.

And the next time you're in a room and detect an unidentified olfactory offense, remember: the quietest ones can sometimes be the most treacherous!

Chapter 7:
The Loudest Trumpet:
World records and incredible fart feats

The world has seen many unique records, including those in the realm of flatulence. Let's explore some of the most astonishing fart feats.

Sound:
The sound of a fart is caused by vibrations in the rectal opening, influenced by the tightness of sphincter muscles and the amount of gas released.

The Guinness World Record:
While there are conflicting reports, the most frequently cited record for the loudest fart is 113 decibels, comparable to the noise level at a rock concert. This record was allegedly set by Herkimer Chort of Ripley, NY, USA, in 1972.

Duration Domination:
The world record for the longest continuous fart is held by Paul Hunn, achieved in 2009. His remarkable fart lasted two minutes and twenty-two seconds, witnessed by an audience and experts.

These records highlight the surprisingly impressive capabilities of the human body in this humorous and natural bodily function.

The Musical Maestros:

Throughout history, there have been individuals known for their unique ability to control and manipulate their flatulence, turning it into a veritable art form. The most famous of these was "Le Pétomane," a French performer in the late 1800s and early 1900s, who entertained audiences with his controlled toots, producing sounds ranging from tiny whispers to thunderous blasts.

Fart Fireworks:

It's a risky feat and not recommended, but there are those who've attempted to light their farts, producing a short-lived blue flame. The science behind it? Methane, a component of human gas, is flammable.

The Silent Marathon:

There are tales of individuals who've managed to silently release gas for an entire dinner or meeting without anyone noticing, making it an unofficial "stealth" record of its own.

Global Fart Championships:
Believe it or not, there are actual competitions around the world where participants vie for titles like "longest," "loudest," and "most musical" fart. Some of these events even raise money for charity, proving that with a little humor, even flatulence can serve a good cause.

Cinematic Celebrations:
The world of film hasn't shied away from highlighting monumental fart moments. Movies like "**Blazing Saddles**" have showcased iconic fart scenes that have since become a part of pop culture history.

The Science of Sound:
The loudness and timbre of a fart depend on several factors, including the amount of gas, its speed of release, and the tension of the anal sphincter. Those who can manipulate these factors just right can produce a vast range of sounds, from the subtle 'pfft' to the roaring 'BRAAAP.'

The world of fart records is as diverse as it is humorous. From individuals seeking to etch their names in history with a resounding toot to charitable events that leverage the universal humor of flatulence, the human desire to laugh, celebrate, and occasionally compete with our natural bodily functions remains a testament to our playful spirit. So, the next time you feel the wind gathering, remember you might just be on the precipice of making history!

Chapter 8:
Farting Fauna: Animals that fart and the role of flatulence in the animal kingdom

Humans aren't the only ones who pass wind. The animal kingdom is rife with creatures that let it rip, from the depths of the ocean to the vastness of the savannah. This chapter takes you on a whirlwind tour of the farting fauna, revealing nature's gassiest secrets.

Cows: Methane Machines:

Renowned for their contributions to global methane emissions, cows' four-chambered stomachs produce vast amounts of gas due to their fermentative digestion process. A single cow can release between 70 and 120 kilograms of methane per year!

Horses: Not Far Behind:

Anyone who's spent time in a stable knows that horses can be quite gassy. Their large cecum, an intestinal pouch where hay and other fibers break down, is a significant source of these windy expulsions.

Termites: Tiny but Mighty:
Though small, termites are responsible for a considerable amount of methane release due to the breakdown of cellulose in their diet. In fact, they are among the largest natural sources of methane emissions in the world.

Fish: Underwater Wind:
Certain fish species, especially herrings, communicate and navigate in the dark by emitting bubbles of gas. The bubbles make a sound that's detectable by other fish, essentially creating an underwater fart language.

Birds: The Non-Farters:
Interestingly, most birds don't fart. Their digestive systems are efficient, and any waste gasses are mixed with other waste to be expelled in one go. However, there are some exceptions, like the ostrich, known to produce notable toots.

Fish: Underwater Farts:

Fish fart. They release gas from their swim bladders to help adjust their buoyancy.

Elephants: Trumpeting Both Ends:

While they might be famous for their trumpeting trunks, elephants also produce sizable farts, thanks to their herbivorous diet rich in fibrous plant material.

Sea Anemones: Silent but Bubbly:

These aquatic creatures expel gas through an orifice that acts as both a mouth and anus. The result? Silent underwater emissions that bubble up to the surface.

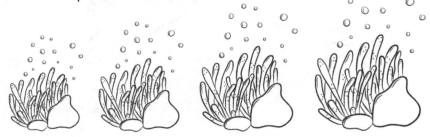

Man's Best Friend:

Dogs can be quite gassy, especially certain breeds. Their farts vary in sound and smell, often influenced by their diet. Feeding them easily digestible foods can help reduce the frequency and potency of their gassy episodes.

Jurassic Farts:

Dinosaurs likely farted too. Some scientists speculate that sauropods (like the Brachiosaurus) produced enough methane to influence prehistoric climates.

The Purpose of Animal Flatulence:
Beyond mere amusement, animal farts serve various functions, from communication and buoyancy control in fish to aiding digestion in herbivores. For many creatures, farting is a vital and natural part of their biology.

The Environmental Impacts:
Animal flatulence, particularly from livestock like cows and sheep, has been recognized as a significant source of methane – a potent greenhouse gas. This has led to scientific studies and innovations to reduce emissions, including specialized diets and even "fart packs" that collect and store the gas.

The realm of farting fauna offers a fascinating look into the diversity of digestive systems and the varied purposes of flatulence in the animal kingdom. Whether it's a minuscule termite emitting more than its weight in gas or a majestic elephant letting out a booming toot, nature's symphony of farts is as essential as it is amusing. So, the next time you're on a nature walk and hear a rustle followed by a familiar sound, remember: we're not alone in our windy endeavors!

Introducing "Farting Animals: Funny Coloring Book"

Step into the hilarious side of nature with "Farting Animals: Funny Coloring Book." From the author of "Fartology," this book brings a light-hearted touch to animal flatulence through engaging illustrations. Each page offers a chance to add color to the funniest moments of animal life. As a special sneak peek, small sample illustrations from the book are available on this page. Perfect for anyone who enjoys a playful approach to the animal world, this coloring book is not only entertaining but also a great way to relax and learn about animals in a unique way. Grab your copy and unleash your creativity on these comical creatures!

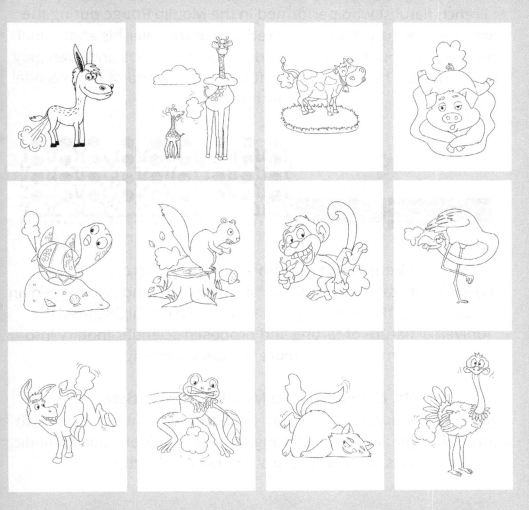

Chapter 9:
Fart-ography: The world's most famous farters and their contribution to toot culture

Throughout history, certain individuals have made their mark not just with their actions and words, but also with their farts. From celebrated performers to influential figures, this chapter delves into those who've elevated flatulence from mere bodily function to cultural phenomenon.

Le Pétomane – The Fartiste:
Joseph Pujol, known by his stage name "Le Pétomane," was a French flatulist who performed in the Moulin Rouge during the late 19th century. With his incredible control over his abdominal muscles, he could produce a wide range of sounds and even play tunes, making him a renowned figure in the world of professional farting.

Benjamin Franklin – Founding Farter:
The eminent statesman, known for his wisdom and wit, penned an essay titled "Fart Proudly." This satirical piece highlighted the universal nature of farting and proposed scientific inquiry into making farts more pleasant-smelling.

Mr. Methane – The Modern-Day Fartiste:
A contemporary performer, Mr. Methane combines comedy with controlled flatulence, performing musical renditions and comedic acts, all centered around the art of farting.

Mozart – A Musical Farter:
The renowned composer Wolfgang Amadeus Mozart had a well-documented sense of humor, particularly about farting. Some of his letters to family members included playful and cheeky references to flatulence.

Emperor Claudius – The Decreeing Tooter:
The Roman Emperor Claudius is said to have passed a decree allowing Romans to fart at meal times for good health, highlighting the importance of expelling wind for one's well-being.

Howard Stern – Broadcasting the Toot:
The radio host has never shied away from the topic of flatulence. Over the years, he's included numerous fart-themed segments, interviews, and contests, cementing the fart's place in modern pop culture.

Famous Fart Scenes in Cinema:
From "Blazing Saddles" to "Dumb and Dumber," cinema has had its fair share of iconic fart scenes. These moments, while comedic, also underscore the universal and relatable nature of flatulence.

The annals of fart history are rich with figures who've either embraced, celebrated, or inadvertently found themselves in the limelight due to their gassy episodes. From ancient emperors to modern-day performers, the influence of these individuals serves as a testament to the enduring cultural relevance and universal humor of farts. In the grand tapestry of human achievement, the threads of flatulence weave a tale both hilarious and profoundly human.

Chapter 11:
Fartlek Training: The (un)expected intersection of exercise and flatulence

The world of fitness is filled with surprising moments, and sometimes, it's not just your muscles that are getting a workout. From the well-known 'runner's trots' to the hilarious moments in a yoga class, let's jog (and jiggle) through the gassy world of physical exertion.

Introduction to Fartlek:
Fartlek, a Swedish term meaning "speed play", is a training method that blends continuous running with interval training. It might sound funny, but the name has nothing to do with farts! However, the unpredictable nature of this training can mirror our unpredictable bodily functions.

Runner's Trots:
Many long-distance runners are all too familiar with the sudden urge to use the restroom during a run. This phenomenon, known as the "runner's trots", is caused by increased intestinal activity during physical activity.

Abdominal Workouts – The Pressure Cookers:
Crunches, leg raises, and other core exercises put pressure on the abdomen, often leading to an unplanned release. It's the body's natural way of making space, so embrace the toot and move on!

Aerobics & Jumping – Shake, Rattle, and Roll:
The continuous movement and jumping in aerobics can shake things up internally, leading to some bubbly surprises. It's a sign that you're giving it your all.

Deep Breathing – The Oxygen Effect:
Deep and forceful breathing, especially during exercises like pilates or intense cardio, can lead to swallowing air, which has to find its way out eventually, often leading to both burping and farting.

Weightlifting – Pushing More Than Just Weights:
The strain and exertion of lifting heavy weights can sometimes lead to an unexpected release of gas. It's a testament to the effort and energy being put into the lift.

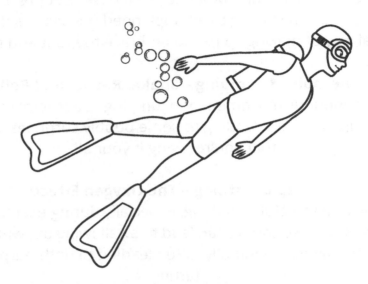

Swimming – Bubbles Below:
The pressure difference in water, combined with the body movements during swimming, can lead to the release of gas bubbles. It's a natural buoyancy aid!

Pre-Exercise Meals – Fueling More Than Just Muscles:
Certain pre-workout meals can increase gas production, especially foods high in fiber or certain proteins. Timing and food choice can be key to a gas-free workout.

Embracing the Unexpected:
The truth is, everyone, no matter how fit, has experienced a workout toot. Instead of feeling embarrassed, it's essential to remember that it's a natural bodily function and often a sign that your body is engaged and working hard.

Physical exertion and bodily functions go hand in hand. Whether you're a seasoned athlete or someone just starting on their fitness journey, understanding and embracing the gassy moments can lead to a more relaxed and enjoyable workout experience. After all, a fart is just your body's way of giving you a round of applause!

Chapter 12:
Gone with the Wind: Memorable farts in literature, cinema, and popular culture

Art imitates life, and life, as we know, comes with its fair share of flatulent moments. From the earliest comedic tales to modern-day silver screen hilarities, the universal experience of farting has often been portrayed in arts and culture. Let's take a whimsical journey through some of the most memorable gas-passing moments in history.

The Literary Legacies:
Authors, from Rabelais to Mark Twain, have occasionally punctuated their prose with a comical fart, reminding readers of the humor in human nature. For instance, Geoffrey Chaucer's "The Miller's Tale" in "The Canterbury Tales" features a fart so significant it plays a pivotal role in the plot.

Farts in Film:
There's no shortage of fart jokes and scenes in movies. Mel Brooks' "Blazing Saddles" set the gold standard with its infamous campfire scene, and the resonance of such scenes has ensured that the legacy continues in modern comedies.

TV Toots:
From animated series like "South Park" and "Family Guy" to live-action shows, flatulence has found its moment in the spotlight, usually amidst roaring audience laughter.

Musical Moments:
Classical composer Joseph Haydn wrote a string quartet (Op. 33 No. 2) nicknamed "The Joke", which includes some cheeky musical imitation of a fart. Modern music hasn't shied away either, with numerous artists incorporating flatulence for both comedic and serious effects.

Artistic Interpretations:
While visual art might not capture the sound or scent of a fart, there are many artworks, both classical and modern, that depict moments of flatulence, emphasizing its universality across ages and cultures.

Famous Farting Personalities:
From emperors like Claudius, who legalized farting at banquets, to celebrities candidly sharing their gassy tales, flatulence has been a democratic experience shared by people from all walks of life.

Farts in Folklore:
Many cultures have tales and legends that incorporate flatulence. From mischievous spirits blamed for nightly toots to stories where farts play pivotal roles in teaching life lessons, these tales are both amusing and illuminating.

Comedy Shows & Stand-ups:
Numerous comedians have incorporated fart anecdotes and jokes into their routines, drawing laughter from audiences who see their own experiences reflected in the stories.

Memes and the Internet:
The digital age has seen the rise of fart-related memes, GIFs, and videos. A simple search can lead to hours of laughter, proving once again the universal comedic value of flatulence.

Pop Culture Products:
From whoopee cushions to fart-scented candles, the market is filled with products designed to emulate or celebrate the humor of flatulence, highlighting its ingrained position in our collective culture.

Throughout history, art and culture have held a mirror to our lives, capturing every aspect of the human experience.

Farts, though sometimes seen as taboo, are a universal part of this experience. Their frequent portrayal in various mediums, from literature to cinema, underscores their enduring appeal and the shared understanding of the humor they bring. As we look back, it's evident: farts are not just a fleeting moment but have left an indelible mark on the winds of time.

Chapter 13:
Farts in the Future: Speculation on the evolution of human flatulence and space-age solutions for smelly situations

As we rocket into the future, with visions of interstellar travel and high-tech lives, one might wonder how our most natural, humorous, and sometimes inconvenient bodily function will fare. Will we engineer odorless farts? Will astronauts have special suits to deal with flatulence in zero gravity? Let's speculate!

Evolutionary Emissions:
Just as our diets and lifestyles have evolved over millennia, there's a possibility that the composition and frequency of our farts might change based on our future diets and environments. Will a pill replace beans as the primary gas producer?

Odorless Utopia:
With advances in biotechnology, we might develop probiotics or dietary supplements that alter our gut flora to produce fragrance-free flatulence. Perfumed toots, anyone?

Spacesuit Squeakers:
In the zero-gravity environment of space, gasses behave differently. Future spacesuit designs might incorporate venting systems to safely release astronaut flatulence or even harness it as a minor propulsion method.

Environmental Impacts:
Could we harness the methane from human farts as a miniature renewable energy source? Though minor in comparison to other sources, every bit counts!

Silent Alerts:
With wearable tech becoming increasingly advanced, we might see the development of underwear that alerts us of an impending fart, allowing us to choose the ideal moment to release.

The AI Fart Analyst:
Future smart toilets or wearable tech might analyze our farts for health insights. An irregular toot could prompt an alert to adjust our diet or check for potential health issues.

Farts in Futuristic Art:
As art evolves, we might see holographic fart displays, interactive fart museums, or even musical compositions based entirely on synthesized toots of different pitches and durations.

Galactic Gas:
Imagine meeting extraterrestrial life. How do they perceive or experience flatulence? Cross-species fart communication might be an amusing, if unlikely, scenario.

Ultimate Fart Control:
Through muscle training or advanced tech, we might achieve the dream of controlling the timing, sound, and scent of every fart, turning each one into a masterful, deliberate expression.

As we journey into the realms of future possibilities, it's amusing to think about how one of our most basic bodily functions will adapt or be adapted. Whether through biotechnological advances or the challenges of space travel, the humble fart is set to embark on an exciting, and undoubtedly humorous, journey into the unknown.

Farts in the Future

Chapter 14:
Toot Tunes: Famous songs, jingles, and musical masterpieces inspired by the humble fart

Music has never shied away from humor, the taboo, or the downright silly. Across ages and cultures, the universal act of farting has made its way into melodies, rhythms, and even the occasional symphonic movement. However, prepare for an unconventional journey - the contents of this chapter are fun, creative speculations and imaginings that play with the concept of 'musical farts'. Embark on a melodious journey through the world of musical flatulence, where fact blends with fiction in the spirit of good fun.

The Whoopee Waltz:
A hypothetical dance number from the early 20th century, this whimsical tune might have accompanied the popular whoopee cushion's debut, urging dancers to laugh off any unexpected sounds.

Folkloric Flatulence:
Many folk songs from around the world humorously address the natural human act of farting. From playful tunes to stories where the toot takes center stage, the tradition of singing about gas is age-old.

Modern Pop and Pops:
Some pop artists have cheekily incorporated fart sounds or themes into their songs, either as a comedic element or a nod to the universal human experience.

The Classic "Fart Sonata":
While not mainstream, the idea of a classical piece mimicking the sounds and rhythms of various farts could serve as a humorous interlude in a typically serious symphony.

Jingles and Ad Tunes:
Modern commercials, especially those for products related to digestion or gas relief, have leveraged catchy jingles that allude to or directly reference the act of farting.

The Jazz "Jazzercise" Fizz:
Imagine a playful jazz number where the trumpets mimic fart sounds, turning them into a melody, allowing audiences to find humor in the unexpected.

Rock & Roll Rumbles:
Rock has always been about pushing boundaries. A song that humorously celebrates the rebellious nature of a loud fart could very well have its place in rock history.

The Lullaby of the Silent Toot:
A soft, playful tune designed for children, teaching them about the body's natural functions in a light-hearted way.

Techno Toots:

In the digital age, music creators have all sorts of sounds at their fingertips. A track where synthesized fart sounds become the core rhythm could be both amusing and oddly catchy.

Operatic Overtones:

An over-the-top opera scene where a dramatic moment is interrupted (or punctuated) by an unexpected toot could add humor to an otherwise serious performance.

From the delicate sounds of classical strings to the pulsing beats of electronic dance music, the fart has found its musical moments. As we appreciate the myriad ways in which artists have embraced this comical aspect of human nature, it becomes evident that farts, in all their sonorous glory, hold a unique and endearing place in the world of music.

Chapter 15.
Gas-tronomy Delights: Recipes for the brave, aimed at creating the mightiest of toots

For those gastronomes who believe that a hearty meal should be followed by an equally hearty toot, this chapter is a tribute to you. Here, we present dishes that are not only delicious but also guaranteed to stoke the fires of your digestive symphony.

The Bean Bonanza Soup:
The main ingredient, beans, known as the 'musical fruit', makes this soup a flatulence powerhouse. Combined with broccoli and cabbage, this trifecta ensures an eventful aftermath.

Lactose Lover's Creamy Pasta:
For those sensitive to lactose, this rich, cheesy pasta dish with a base of full-fat cream is sure to produce some resonant results.

Carbonated Cauliflower Curry:
Cauliflower, a cruciferous vegetable, teams up with fizzy soda in this curry. The carbonation adds a bubbly zest to the dish and your digestion.

Jerusalem Artichoke & Asparagus Stir-fry:
Both these ingredients contain fructans and oligosaccharides which can be gas-producing in the gut. Paired together, they create a delightful dish with a potent aftermath.

Lactose-Induced Laughter:
Rich in lactose, dairy products like milk and cheese are infamous for inducing gas. They're a delight for the taste buds but can lead to notable flatulence, especially for those with lactose intolerance. This is due to lactose fermenting in the gut. A meal rich in creamy cheeses promises a humorous, gassy aftermath.

Mighty Methane Muffins:
A delightful dessert made with a blend of whole grains, fibrous fruits like apples and pears, and sweetened with sugar alcohols like xylitol or sorbitol which can contribute to gassiness.

Gas-tastic Garlic and Onion Guacamole:
Both garlic and onion can cause gas. Mash them with avocados, which contain sorbitol, and you have a trio of toot-inducing ingredients.

Fart-forward Fermented Kimchi:
Fermented foods are known for their beneficial probiotics but can also induce gas. This spicy Korean cabbage dish promises a combination of zest and zestiness.

Apricot and Prune Pudding:
These fruits are not only delicious but contain natural sugars and fibers that can lead to a gassy aftermath. This pudding is a sweet end to a meal, with a potentially noisy encore.

Carbonara with a Soda Pop:
Pair a creamy, rich carbonara with a carbonated drink of your choice. The combination of dairy and bubbles is sure to provide an aural treat later on.

In the world of gastronomy, every culinary choice has its reaction, and these recipes are designed to amplify it. It's all in good fun, of course. Remember, while indulging in these delightful dishes, it's all about balance. Too much of anything can be overwhelming, even in the world of toots.

Enjoy responsibly and always be ready with a cheeky grin and a good-natured shrug. After all, everyone knows that laughter is the best digestive aid!

Chapter 16:
The Fart-chive: Memorable fart anecdotes and stories submitted by readers

From embarrassing public toots to heartwarming wind-breaking moments, our readers have shared their most memorable fart tales. Here's a compilation of those stories, proving once again that farts, in all their unpredictable glory, are a universal experience we all share.

Elevator Escapade by Raj K.:
In a packed elevator, I felt a silent one coming. Thinking it'd be odorless, I let it slide. But oh, how wrong I was! By the fourth floor, everyone knew. By the fifth, they were all looking at each other. I exited the elevator on the sixth, but not before hearing a kid say, 'Mommy, it smells like broccoli!'

First Date Flatulence by Chloe B.:

On my first date with my now-husband, I accidentally let one out while laughing. Instead of being embarrassed, he responded with one of his own, twice as loud. We knew then that we were meant to be.

Toot during Tadasana by Aman S.:

During a yoga class, as I stretched into the mountain pose, I accidentally released a mountainous toot. The worst part? It was a quiet meditation session. The best part? The instructor said, 'And release all that doesn't serve you.' Everyone chuckled.

The Conference Call Catastrophe by Nora J.:

I was on a serious business video call. Thinking my microphone was on mute, I let out a relief fart. It wasn't silent. My boss paused and said, 'Well, that's one way to comment on the quarterly results!'

Beach Blast by Pedro L.:

While lying belly-down on an inflatable at the beach, I let out a fart. The vibration and the sound were amplified. A nearby kid shouted, 'Look, mom, a jet ski!'

Symphony of Sounds by Mei Y.:
At a family dinner, my grandpa, known for his love for beans, began his fart symphony. As we tried not to laugh, my little niece conducted his performance using her fork and knife, making it a night to remember.

Romantic Resonance by Jamal R.:
Proposing to my girlfriend under the stars, just as I knelt and opened the ring box, a nervous toot betrayed me. She giggled and said, 'If you promise to keep making me laugh like this, yes!'

School Slip-up by Amy P.:
In a silent classroom during an exam, my stomach grumbled, leading to an unexpected fart. The boy next to me, trying to be chivalrous, exclaimed, 'Excuse me!' taking the blame. We've been best friends ever since.

These tales from the Fart-chive remind us that while farts might be unpredictable and sometimes embarrassing, they also lead to laughter, memories, and even new friendships. They're a natural part of life, and as these stories show, sometimes they come at the most unexpected times - but always leave a lasting impression.

Chapter 17:
The DIY Wind Workshop: Fun and safe experiments related to farts for readers to try at home

Have you ever been curious about the science behind farts? Or perhaps just in the mood for some light-hearted, fart-related fun? This chapter dives into DIY experiments that you can safely try at home to explore the magical world of flatulence. Let the wind experiments begin!

The Balloon Bloat:
Materials:
Balloon
Small funnel
Baking soda
Vinegar
Experiment:

Pour a tablespoon of baking soda into the balloon using the funnel. Fill a bottle with vinegar about a quarter of the way. Attach the balloon's opening to the bottle's mouth without letting the baking soda in. When ready, lift the balloon, allowing the baking soda to fall into the vinegar. Watch the balloon inflate due to the gas produced – similar to how certain foods produce gas in our stomachs!

Gas Jar:
Materials:
A jar
Warm water
Sugar
Active dry yeast
Experiment:

Fill the jar with warm water, then add a packet of active dry yeast and a teaspoon of sugar. Close the lid. Yeast will consume the sugar and produce carbon dioxide. You'll see bubbles rise, much like the gas in our intestines!

Farty Party Drink:
Materials:
Lemon juice
Water
Baking soda
A glass.

Experiment:
Mix lemon juice and water in a glass. Slowly add a teaspoon of baking soda. Listen and watch the fizzy reaction. This illustrates how acid in our stomach reacts with certain foods producing gas.

Flameless Fart:
Materials:
Soap solution (water + dish soap)
Straw
Tray

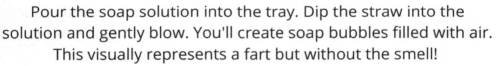

Experiment:
Pour the soap solution into the tray. Dip the straw into the solution and gently blow. You'll create soap bubbles filled with air. This visually represents a fart but without the smell!

Stink-o-Meter:
Materials:
Different types of food
(beans, cabbage,
cheese, carbonated drink)
Notebook
Brave nose

Experiment:
Consume one type of food and note the time. Document every time you pass gas and rate the smell on a scale of 1-10. It's a fun way to discover which foods make your toots more potent.

Sound Scale:
Materials: **Air-filled balloons of various sizes**
Experiment:
Release air from each balloon, trying to mimic the sound of a fart.
Notice how different sizes and air pressures create varying
sounds. This demonstrates how the volume of intestinal gas can
affect the sound of a fart.

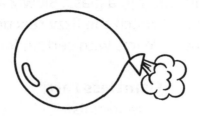

These experiments provide a light-hearted way to understand the
concept of gas production and release, both inside our bodies and
in the environment around us. Plus, it's always fun to mimic the
sounds and sights of farts in unexpected ways, so gather your
materials, get curious, and let the wind blow! Always remember
safety first and ensure proper supervision for younger
participants.

Chapter 18:
A Pocket Guide to Fart Jokes: An anthology of the best fart jokes out there

There's a term called "flatulence humor". It's been around since ancient times and is considered one of the oldest forms of comedy. Farts are universally funny. Across cultures and ages, the simple act of passing gas has given rise to chuckles, giggles, and full-blown belly laughs.

For those moments when you need a quick joke to lighten the mood, here's a pocket guide packed with some of the best fart jokes out there!

Why should you never fart on an elevator?
It's wrong on so many levels.

What do you get if you eat beans and onions?
Tear gas!

What do you call someone who doesn't like the sound of a fart?
A lack-toot intolerant.

What do you call a cat that eats beans?
Puss-toot!

Why are farts like children?
You're always proud of your own!

What did the maxi pad say to the fart?
You are the wind beneath my wings.

What did the fart say after a hard day's work?
"I'm pooped!"

Why don't scientists trust farts?
Because they can't be seen, only smelled.

What's a fart's favorite instrument?
The trumpet.

Why did the fart go to school?
To improve its "scent-sibility."

What do you call a room full of people trying to hold in farts?
A silent but deadly conference.

Why was the fart acting so humble?
It didn't want to be "poot" on a pedestal.

Why do farts smell?
So deaf people can enjoy them too!

What's invisible and smells like bananas?
A fart from a monkey.

How can you tell if a calendar is popular?
If its days are "numbered" from too many fart jokes.

Why don't farts graduate from school?
They always end up getting expelled.

What's a fart's favorite game?
Blow and seek.

What do you call a person who doesn't fart in public?
A private toot-or.

Why did the fart go near the cash register?
It wanted to smell the "scents."

Why did the tomato turn red?
Because it saw the salad dressing...
and the lettuce let out a little fart.

How do you make a tissue dance?
Put a little "boogie" in it. And if you're lucky,
it might let out a toot!

What did the left butt cheek say to the right one?
Between you and me, things might get a bit noisy.

Why are farts smart?
Because they always "pass" the test!

What's a fart's favorite drink?
Carbonated soda, for those bubbly moments.

Why was the fart arrested?
It was a "smelly-tant" to laughter!

What's a fart's favorite weather?
A little wind!

Why did the fart apologize?
It didn't mean to come out that way.

Why did the fart go on a date with the burp?
They just clicked!

What did the butt say after a big meal?
That was gas-tastic!

Why was the fart feeling down?
It felt passed over.

What do you call a group of musical farts?
A toot ensemble!

How do you describe a vegetarian's fart?
Plant-based poot!

What's a polite fart's favorite song?
"Excuse Me" by Janet Jackson.

Why did the fart blush?
Because it came out in the open.

How can you make a fart smell better?
Put a little "poot-pourri" on it!

Why was the fart so mysterious?
It was a silent but deadly secret agent.

What do you get when you cross a snake and a pie?
A python!

Why did the bicycle stand on its own?
Because it's "two-tired" of all the fart jokes!

What's a ghost's favorite way to pass gas?
Boo-toots!

Why did the can of beans write a letter?
To air its grievances.

How do farts communicate?
By air mail!

Why was the fart so proud?
Because it was "the bomb."

What do you call a cat that can play the trumpet?
A tooty tabby!

Why did the scarecrow keep farting?
Because he was out-standing in his field!

Why did the fart go to therapy?
It felt suppressed!

What's a mathematician's favorite kind of fart?
A "pi"-roo!

Why did the fart smell sweet?
It was a dessert toot!

What did one fart bubble say to the other in the bath?
"I think we're in hot water!"

How do you make a tissue fart?
Sneezing!

Why did the fart break up with the burp?
It felt taken for granted.

Why did the astronaut refuse to fart in space?
Didn't want to become a gas giant!

What do you call someone who derives pleasure from the flatulence of others?
A "fart connoisseur."

Why did the fart fail the lie detector test?
It was too airy.

How does a queen fart?
Nobly.

What did the fart say to the echo?
"Stop copying me!"

Why was the fart such a good friend?
Always had your back.

What genre do fart stories belong to?
Gas-tales!

Why was the fart feeling ambitious?
It wanted to be a whistle!

Why did the butt go to college?
To get a little behind in its studies!

What's a fart's favorite exercise?
"Pass" the parcel!

Why don't farts go to the doctor?
They can't stomach the wait!

What's a fart's least favorite song?
"Wind Beneath My Wings."

How do you make a romantic fart?
Add a bit of "rose scent."

Farts, in all their smelly glory, have always had comedic potential. Whether you're in the mood to share a silly joke with friends or just want a reason to giggle on a gloomy day, these fart jokes are sure to bring a smile to your face. Remember, life is always better when you're laughing... even if it's about something as cheeky as a toot!

Chapter 19:
The Grand Finale: A fictional (and hilarious) account of the world's most important fart-off competition.

Enjoy this hilarious fictional fart-filled tale taking place in the bubbling city of Gasstonville!

In the bustling city of Gasstonville, there was an annual event that drew crowds from near and far. The Great Gas-Off, as it was affectionately known, was a competition of epic proportions. It was where masters of the art of flatulence came to showcase their talents. It wasn't just about noise or duration. Oh no, this was about style, creativity, and an olfactory experience that would be remembered for generations.

This year was particularly exciting because the reigning champion, Sir Poots-a-Lot,was going head-to-head with a newcomer, the mysterious Miss Toot'n'Flee. Rumors swirled about her ability to toot tunes of popular songs and even her knack for creating scents that were oddly familiar.

The stage was set, and as the sun set, the massive stadium, known as the Gas-o drome, was filled to the brim. Commentators Wendy Windbottom and BarryBlasterson were ready, microphones in hand.
"Ladies and gentlemen, welcome to the Great Gas-Off! Today we will witness history!" Barry announced.

Sir Poots-a-Lot was first. Dressed in his signature velvet robe, he took the stage with grace. With a confident smirk, he launched into his routine. His farts flowed like a symphony, varying in pitch and tone, creating a medley of familiar classical tunes.

The audience clapped along, some even shedding tears at the sheer beauty of it. The grand finale was a thunderous crescendo that seemed to shake the very foundation of the Gas-o-drome.

Miss Toot'n'Flee, on the other hand, brought props. She had a bouquet of flowers,scented candles, and even a table with a romantic dinner setting. With a wink to the crowd, she began. Each fart was expertly timed, not just with the tune she was creating, but also with an action. A romantic tune was accompanied by the scent of roses, much to the astonishment of the audience.

She even managed to mimic the scent of the roast chicken dinner on the table,causing the audience to burst into fits of laughter. Her grand finale was a rendition of the current hit pop song and the smell? Freshly baked cookies.

Wendy Windbottom was in stitches, "is truly revolutionary!" I've never seen anything like it! Miss Toot'n'Flee

As the judges deliberated, the tension was palpable. Finally, they emerged with their decision. In a surprise twist, they announced a tie! Both Sir Poots-a-Lot and Miss Toot'n'Flee had brought something unique to the table.

The Gas-o-drome erupted in cheers. It wasn't about winning or losing; it was about celebrating the hilarious and wondrous world of farts. And as the crowd left, many were heard saying that this was, without a doubt, the best Great Gas-Off in history.

And so, in the heart of Gasstonville, legends were made, laughter was shared, and the world of competitive farting would never be the same again.

The End!

Made in the USA
Monee, IL
22 November 2023

47111858R00037